ABOUT THE BANK STREET READY-TO-READ SERIES

Seventy years of educational research and innovative teaching have given the Bank Street College of Education the reputation as America's most trusted name in early childhood education.

Because no two children are exactly alike in their development, we have designed the *Bank Street Ready-to-Read* series in three levels to accommodate the individual stages of reading readiness of children ages four through eight.

- *Level 1:* GETTING READY TO READ—read-alouds for children who are taking their first steps toward reading.
- *Level 2:* READING TOGETHER—for children who are just beginning to read by themselves but may need a little help.
- *Level 3:* I CAN READ IT MYSELF—for children who can read independently.

Our three levels make it easy to select the books most appropriate for a child's development and enable him or her to grow with the series step by step. The *Bank Street Ready-to-Read* books also overlap and reinforce each other, further encouraging the reading process.

We feel that making reading fun and enjoyable is the single most important thing that you can do to help children become good readers. And we hope you'll be a part of Bank Street's long tradition of learning through sharing.

The Bank Street College of Education

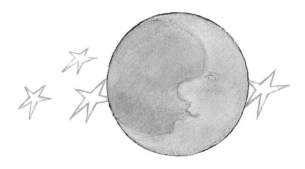

To May Garelick
—B.B.

To my daughter, Ana, and son, Pablo
—J.G.

MOON BOY

A Bantam Little Rooster Book
Simultaneous paper-over-board and trade paper editions/April 1990

Little Rooster is a trademark of Bantam Books,
a division of Bantam Doubleday Dell Publishing Group, Inc.

Series graphic design by Alex Jay/Studio J
Associate Editors: Gwendolyn Smith, Gillian Bucky

Special thanks to James A. Levine, Betsy Gould,
Erin B. Gathrid, and Ana Ubiles.

Library of Congress Cataloging-in-Publication Data
Brenner, Barbara.
Moon boy / by Barbara Brenner ; illustrated by J. Gabán
p. cm. — (Bank Street ready-to-read)
"A Bantam little rooster book."
"A Byron Preiss book."
Summary: A moonbeam comes to life one night
and visits a young boy.
ISBN 0-553-05858-4. — ISBN 0-553-34851-5 (pbk.)
[1. Moon—Fiction. 2. Night—Fiction.]
I. Gabán, Jesús, ill. II. Title. III. Series.
PZ7.B7518Mo 1990
[E]—dc20
89-37775 CIP AC

Published simultaneously in the United States and Canada

Bantam Books are published by Bantam Books, a division of Bantam Doubleday
Dell Publishing Group, Inc. Its trademark, consisting of the words "Bantam Books"
and the portrayal of a rooster, is Registered in U.S. Patent and Trademark Office
and in other countries. Marca Registrada. Bantam Books, 666 Fifth Avenue, New
York, New York 10103.

PRINTED IN THE UNITED STATES OF AMERICA

0 9 8 7 6 5 4 3

Bank Street Ready-to-Read™

Moon Boy

by Barbara Brenner
Illustrated by J. Gabán

A Byron Preiss Book

A BANTAM LITTLE ROOSTER BOOK
NEW YORK · TORONTO · LONDON · SYDNEY · AUCKLAND

It was late.
I couldn't sleep.

I stood at my window
and looked out into the dark.
The stars were far away.

The moon was a gold balloon.

I saw a small streak of light fall.
"Shooting star!"
I said to myself.

Just then a shiny dot
landed on my windowsill.

It grew until it was
a golden stream that turned
into a glowing ball of light.

I watched. The ball became
a body and a face.
It was a boy. Small.
Dressed all in white.

"Who are you?" I asked.
"Moon Boy," he said.
"From where?" I asked.
He said, "From there,"
and pointed to the sky.

The moon was a gold balloon.

Now the moon boy stood
in my hand.
Like a little lamp.
Like a night-light
in the shape of a boy.

We talked,
Moon Boy and I.
We played.
He sailed my Noah's Ark
and hid in my house of blocks.

He flew up to my toy shelf
and sat there, singing.
This is the song he sang:

When the moon is a gold balloon,
moon children come out to play.
They ride the clouds
in golden crowds
along the Milky Way.

But soon the moon
began to fade.
Moon Boy said, "It's time."
"Time for what?" I asked.
"Time to go."

"No! Don't go," I said.
But he flew to the sill
as if to leave me.

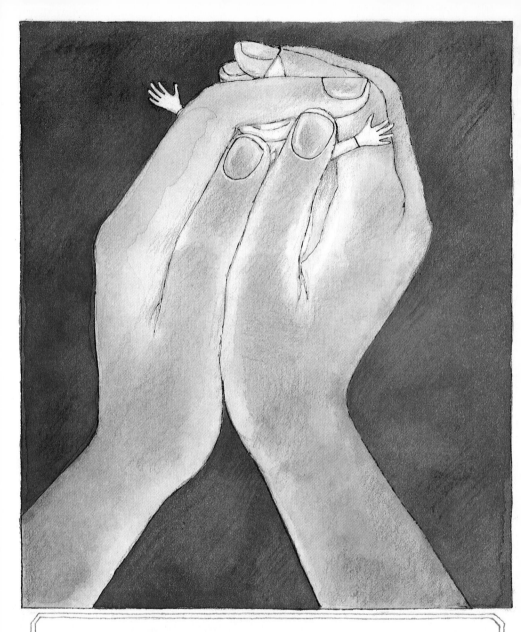

I grabbed him
and held him in my hands.
I spied my toy box,
dropped him in,
and closed the lid tight!

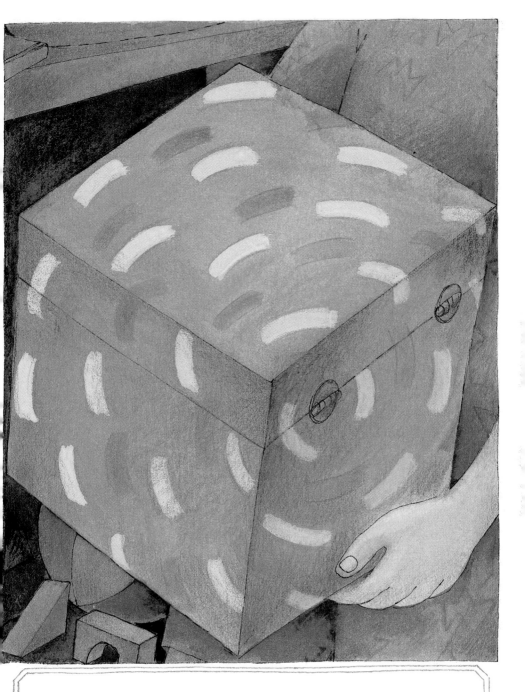

I had him then.
A real moon boy.
To keep like a toy.

But wait . . .
The stars were going out.
The sky turned black.
There was no light.

No moon. No gold balloon.

"What is it?" I cried.
I was afraid.
And then I heard Moon Boy
calling to me from the dark.

"The lights are out
because I am in here.
The moon children
and the stars are sad.

They miss me.
They need me."

I knew then
I would have
to let him go.
A moonbeam is not a toy.
You can't hold it
or lock it in a box.
You need to let it go.

I opened the box
and set the moon boy free.
Once again,

the moon was a gold balloon.

By and by the stars faded.
The moon went in.
I closed my eyes and fell asleep.

In the morning
the sun came out,
and I woke up.
As always.

Barbara Brenner is the author of more than thirty-five books for children, including *Wagon Wheels*, an ALA Notable Book. She writes frequently on subjects related to parenting and is co-author of *Choosing Books for Kids* and *Raising a Confident Child* in addition to being a Senior Editor for the Bank Street College Media Group. Ms. Brenner and her husband, illustrator Fred Brenner, have two sons. They live by a lake in Lords Valley, Pennsylvania.

Jesús Gabán was born in a village near Madrid. He has been illustrating children's books since 1981 and was awarded the Spanish National Prize for Children's Book Illustration in 1984 and 1988. Mr. Gabán's books have been published in Spain, France, Germany, Japan, and the United Kingdom. This is his first book for an American audience.